Milo

Christel van Bourgondië
Tekeningen van Josine van Schijndel

zonnetjes

Zwijsen

De storm

Het stormt op zee.
De golven bonken op de boot.
Wit schuim spat op het dek.
De boot gaat heen en weer.
De visser ziet het.
Zijn boot gaat zinken.
Hij kijkt naar zijn kleine hond.
Die vaart altijd met hem mee.
Hij zet het hondje in een kist.
Die laat hij de zee op glijden.
'Jij redt het vast,' zegt de visser.
'Woef,' blaft het hondje.
Maar dat hoort de visser niet.
De storm raast te hard.
De zee is heel wild.
Hij gooit de kist alle kanten op.
Het hondje duikt in elkaar.
Hij is bang voor de boze zee.
De storm suist om zijn oren.
Tot de zee stil wordt.
En de kist op het strand landt.
Boem!
Het hondje rolt zich op.
Als een klein, nat propje.
De zee zwijgt.

Het is muisstil.
Nu is het hondje bang van de stilte.
Het jankt zachtjes.

De jongen en zijn opa

De jongen loopt over het strand.
Naast hem loopt zijn opa.
Dat doen ze altijd na een storm.
Want de zee werpt van alles op het strand.
Het strand is bezaaid met schuim.
'Er is niets vandaag,' zegt de opa.
'We gaan naar huis.'
'Stil eens, opa,' zegt de jongen.
Hij hoort gejank.
Hij loopt er op af.
Dan ziet hij de kist.
Het hondje lijkt een witte bol.
Met zachte haartjes.
'Arme jij,' zegt de jongen.
'Wat is er met jou gebeurd?'
Het beestje rilt over heel zijn lijf.
De jongen aait over zijn kop.
Het hondje kijkt op.
'Wat ben jij lief,' zegt de jongen.
Hij tilt het hondje op.
En stopt het onder zijn trui.
Daar is het lekker warm.

'Ik noem je Milo,' zegt hij.
Milo is een ander woord voor lief.
En zo krijgt Milo een naam.
En een nieuw baasje.

De jongen gaat vaak naar het strand.
Milo gaat dan mee.
Hij houdt van het strand.
Hij rent de golven in en uit.
Hij begraaft zijn neus in het zand.
Dat is zout en fris.
Het prikt in zijn neus.
Hij stopt zijn neus diep in het zand.
Daar ruikt het naar vroeger.
Naar heel ver weg.
Daar ruikt het fijn.
Wie weet zit er een dik bot!

Milo graaft met zijn poten.
Het zand vliegt alle kanten op.
Zo wild gaat Milo te keer.
De geur wordt steeds sterker.
Ineens voelt Milo iets hards.
'Kijk opa!' roept de jongen.
'Milo heeft wat!'

Opa bekijkt het ding.
'Het is een oude beker,' zegt hij.
'Van goud zo te zien.
Die is vast veel waard.'
Opa aait Milo.
De jongen aait Milo.
'Goed gedaan!'
Thuis krijgt Milo een bot.
Hij kwispelt met zijn staart.
Hij zocht voor zijn vriend een schat.
Nu geeft de jongen hém een schat.
Hij snuffelt er aan.
Hij pakt het bot.
En loopt de tuin in.
Daar begraaft hij het bij een boom.
Diep in de aarde.

9

Milo vindt nog een schat

Ze gaan vaak naar zee.
Steeds wroet Milo in het zand.
Tot hij wat ruikt.
Dan spit hij.
Hij vindt een fles met een boot erin.
Hij vindt een zak met munten.
Hij vindt een armband van zilver.
Elke keer krijgt Milo een bot.

Milo vindt niet zomaar dingen.
Ze zijn oud als de wind.
Ze waren ooit van rijke mensen.
Ze zijn veel geld waard.
'Milo zoekt schatten,' zegt opa.
'Milo is heel speciaal.
Als we hem helpen zoeken,
vinden we vast nog meer.'
Ze gaan elke dag naar het strand.
Met een schep om te graven.
En een kar voor de schatten.
Zo helpen ze Milo.
Ze vinden van alles.
Oude spijkers.
Een ring met een zegel.
Een ketting met een gouden kruis.

Een speld met een parel.
Maar ook een gouden pispot.
En heel veel stukjes hout.
De kuil wordt steeds groter.
De jongen en de opa zien,
dat Milo een schat heeft ontdekt.
Een schat van een piraat.
Misschien wel van Blauwbaard.
Of van Kapitein Haak.

De jongen legt alles in de kar.
Opa rijdt hem naar huis.
Maar een kar met zoveel moois ...
Dat kan niet goed gaan.
Een man met een pet ziet hen.
'Is dat van jullie?' vraagt hij.
Opa zegt: 'Milo vindt schatten.'
'Dat wil ik ook wel,' zegt de man.
Maar opa zegt: 'Die schat is niet van ons.
Hij is voor iemand die er veel van weet.'

De man die er veel van weet,
zegt dat de schat écht oud is.
Alle mensen moeten dit zien.
Hij koopt alles.
Opeens zijn ze rijk,
de jongen en zijn opa.

Er komen mensen van de tv.
De mensen stellen vragen.
De mensen willen Milo zien.
Zo wordt Milo heel erg beroemd.
Milo vindt het best.
Hij krijgt steeds meer botten.
De hele tuin ligt er vol mee.

De boef

De man met de pet denkt:
wat zij kunnen, kan ik ook.
Hij wacht zijn kans af.
Op een nacht sluipt hij naar Milo.
Met een vette kluif in zijn zak.
'Hier Milo,' roept hij zacht.
Zo lokt hij Milo uit zijn hok.
Het bot ruikt heerlijk.
Milo volgt de geur.
Hij loopt recht op de man af.
De man aait Milo.
Hij tilt Milo op.
En zet hem in een doos.
De doos gaat in zijn auto.
Dan gaat hij er snel vandoor.
Zo wordt de man een boef.
De boef rijdt naar een strand.
Een strand ver weg.
Waar niemand Milo kent.
Daar komt de jongen zeker niet.
En er ligt vast een oude schat.
Milo springt blij de auto uit.
Hij ruikt de zee.
Hij hapt naar de golven.
'Hier jij!' roept de boef.

16

'Zoek een schat!'
Maar Milo wil met de golven spelen.
En rondjes rennen.
'Wil je een bot?' vraagt de boef.
'Woef!' blaft Milo.
Dat wil hij wel.
De boef houdt het bot stevig vast.
'Zoek!' roept hij.

Milo laat zijn oren hangen.
Hij snapt er niets van.
Wat een rare man.
Wat moet hij zoeken?
De boef ruikt raar.
Zijn stem is donker en naar.
De boef schopt naar Milo.
Milo springt opzij.
'Zoek, zoek!' roept de boef.
Milo doet niets.
Wat wil die man?
De boef is het zat.
'Bekijk het maar,' zegt hij boos.
Hij neemt Milo mee naar huis.
En sluit hem op in de schuur.
Niemand kan hem horen.
Milo mist de aai van de jongen.
En de lieve woorden van opa.
Hij mist zijn mand bij de kachel,
En de geur van het strand.
Het strand is fijn.
Je ruikt er van alles.
Hij maakt de jongen en opa blij.
En krijgt dan een bot.
Milo mist zijn botten.

De boef trekt zich er niets van aan.
Hij gaat met Milo alle stranden af.
Dan schreeuwt hij:
'Zoek, stom beest!'
Maar hoe Milo ook ruikt.
Hoe hij ook snuft en snuift …
Hij vindt niets.
Op een dag roept de boef boos:
'Aan jou heb ik niets!'
Hij trapt Milo hard.
Milo rolt over de scherpe schelpen.
Hij schaaft zich aan een harde steen.
Zijn poot doet zeer.
Met moeite kan Milo weer opstaan.
Hij kijkt om zich heen.
De boef is weg.
Er is niemand op het strand.
Milo hinkt op drie poten.
Er is niets te eten.
De regen komt.
Milo kan nergens schuilen.
Zijn vacht is smerig en grauw.
Milo sjokt voort over het strand.
De dag wordt nacht.
De nacht wordt dag.
Zo gaat het maar door.
Week in, week uit.

De grootste schat

De jongen mist Milo.
Het is zo stil in huis.
De botten liggen op een hoop.
Hij gooit ze in een kuil.
Net als Milo altijd deed.
Het strand is leeg zonder hond.
Zonder Milo die naar de golven blaft.
Opa hangt foto's op van Milo.
Hij vraagt steeds:
'Heb jij Milo soms gezien?'
Maar Milo is mank en vies.
Wie herkent hem nu nog?
Milo sukkelt over het strand.
Hij rilt van de frisse bries.
Milo eet al dagen niets.
Hij is zo dun als een lat.
Steeds stort hij neer.
Milo heeft niet lang meer te leven.
Hij gaat liggen en denkt:
ik zie de jongen toch niet meer.
En ook zijn opa niet.
Dan ga ik maar dood.
Hij denkt aan zijn mand.
Dicht bij de kachel.

En aan de aai van de jongen.
Dan ziet Milo een kist.
Die lijkt op de kist van de visser.
Hij kruipt erin.
Milo snuft.
Er hangt een geur die hij kent.
Hij legt zijn kop op de bodem.
En sluit zijn ogen.

Zo vinden de jongen en zijn opa hem.
Als een klein, vies propje.
Slapend in een kist.
'Milo!' roept de jongen blij.
'Milo, trouwe vriend,' zegt opa.
Milo slaat zijn ogen op.
Hij kijkt van de jongen naar de opa.
De jongen tilt Milo op.
En stopt hem onder zijn trui.
Met een zucht van genot kruipt Milo dicht
tegen hem aan.
Nu komt het toch nog goed.

De jongen zegt:
'Ik laat je nooit meer gaan.'
'Er is maar één echte schat.
En dat ben jij!'
Zo is het maar net, denkt Milo.

Jij bent mijn grootste schat.

Milo graaft nooit meer in het zand.
Maar hij houdt nog wel van de zee.
Én van de jongen en zijn opa.

Zonnetje bij kern 7 van Veilig leren lezen

1. Het geheim van oma Sien
Geertje Gort en Pauline Oud

2. Milo
Christel van Bourgondië en Josine van Schijndel

3. De schat van opa
Anton van der Kolk en Harmen van Straaten

NEDERLANDSE
KINDERJURY
2007

ISBN 90.276.0096.1
NUR 287
1e druk 2006

© 2006 Tekst: Christel van Bourgondië
© 2006 Illustraties: Josine van Schijndel
Vormgeving: Rob Galema
© Uitgeverij Zwijsen B.V., Tilburg

Voor België:
Zwijsen-Infoboek, Meerhout
D/1919//2006/209

CELEBRATION STORIES

The
Dragon
Doorway

CLARE BEVAN

Illustrated by Trevor Parkin

HODDER
Wayland

Chinese New Year

The Chinese New Year takes place in January
or February, when the new moon arrives.

Each family gathers to welcome its Kitchen
God, who has been visiting Heaven. Everyone
hopes he has given them a glowing report! The
house is made spotlessly clean, people wear
their best clothes, and fire-crackers protect the
doorways from demons.

In China there is a legend that long ago there
lived a cruel monster called Nin. For most of the
year Nin was trapped in a cave, but when winter
ended the monster was allowed to prowl free.
One bitter day it met a little girl dressed in red –
but instead of eating her, Nin scampered away in
terror. Later, the people found out that Nin was
also afraid of loud noises.

The Chinese believe that red is a lucky colour.
At New Year, red is everywhere – the colour of
happiness and good fortune.

Special foods are eaten to celebrate the occasion – sticky rice-cakes called *nin go*; savoury turnip rice-cakes, and orange fruits. Best of all, the children are given red packets with a gift of money inside to reward good behaviour.

Finally, there is a joyful procession through the streets, when the animal of the year makes its appearance. There are noisy bands and fireworks to frighten away bad spirits, or Nin, while silky dragons and dancing lions bring long life and good fortune.

"Kung Hei Fat Choy!" the people call. It means "May you grow rich". The New Year has begun.

The Quest

Nathan sifted through the heap of leaflets on the doormat. All useless of course – except for the one from Quester's Quality Coach Company: *BEAT THOSE WINTER BLUES*, it announced. *Win a family ticket for our February Mystery Tour. Just solve this puzzle to become the lucky winner.*

"Listen to this!" yelled Nathan, racing into the kitchen and reading out the riddle:

Find the Land of the Twittering Sparrows,
Where Dragons have Legs by the Score,
Where Lions will dance for Good Fortune,
Where Fire-crackers hang by the door,
Where Red is the Happiest Colour,
Where Kumquats are Brightest and Best,
Then tell me the Name of the Future
To show you've completed my Quest.

Mum, Dad and Little Maggie stared at him sadly.

"Forget it, son," said Dad with a sigh. "Even if we guessed the right answer, we still wouldn't win. Nothing's been going right for us lately."

Nathan knew that was true. This was the most miserable January anyone in the family could remember. Dad had slipped off his new jogging machine and broken his big toe. Mum had lost her pantomime job (as 'Goldy the Magic Chicken') because the feathers gave her a rash. The roof was leaking, the washing machine was chewing holes in the clothes, and Little Maggie was giving everyone her very gungy cold.

"Pop to the village, love," croaked Mum, sneezing over her slice of burnt toast, "and buy me a packet of cough sweets."

"See if you can bring home some good luck, too," groaned Dad. "We could do with it."

But Nathan had already escaped from the House of Gloom.

Nathan still had the puzzling poem in his hand, so he repeated the words to himself as he trudged to the local shops. "*The Land of the Twittering Sparrows?* That could be England. Or France. Or anywhere. And how many legs are dragons supposed to have?"

He bought the cough sweets and was wandering home again when he spotted a poster on the travel agent's door. It showed a dragon-headed boat full of jolly Vikings, and said: *Norway's The Answer.*

That's a dragon with lots of legs, thought Nathan. But are there any lions in Norway? I'd better ask inside.

A woman looked up from her desk. "Can I help you?" she asked.

"I hope so," said Nathan, showing her the verse. "Any ideas?"

The woman gulped and shook her head. "It's my first day," she said anxiously. "I only know about Disneyland. And I've never met a kumquat, either."

"Thanks, anyway," said Nathan, nipping outside again.

Nathan crossed the road and stopped beside a mountain of dog baskets. Maybe Pet Shop Pete would know.

"Ever heard of a dancing lion?" Nathan called out to Pete.

Pete peered round a maze of hamster cages. "Nope," he said. "But I once sold a parrot who could roller-skate…"

Nathan grinned at Pete, then followed the path to the library.

There was a long queue of grumpy people waiting for the computer, so Nathan tried the geography section instead. Shelf after shelf of enormous books! The answer had to be in here somewhere. But where on earth should he begin?

"Can I help you?" demanded the frosty-looking librarian.

Nathan took a deep breath. "Twittering Sparrows?" he asked, hopefully.

"Try the bird books," she snapped. "And we close in five minutes."

Nathan shrugged and crept away. Dad was probably right. The whole thing was a complete waste of time. He might as well take the short-cut home.

Nathan zigzagged through the market, then paused. Maybe he should buy Little Maggie a treat from the fruit stall? Apples, or grapes, or...

"What are these?"asked Nathan, pointing at a pyramid of tiny, bite-sized oranges.

"Kumquats," grumbled Fred, the fruit seller. "And you can have a free sample. No one else seems to want them."

"Thanks!" gasped Nathan. "But where do they come from? Africa? Spain?"

"Off the lorry. Fresh this morning," growled Fred, shoving a handful into a paper bag. "You eat the skin and they make your lips sore." Then he swung round to serve another customer.

Nathan headed for the charity shop. This was his favourite window, always stacked with second-hand surprises. He gazed at the crazy collection of junk as he sank his teeth into one of the shiny fruits. The skin was soft and sharp. The juice was sweet and sour. "Wow!" he murmured. "Better than sherbet."

And then he saw the dragon.

The Scarlet Cupboard

The painted creature glittered like gold, and it crawled down the doors of a scarlet cupboard that stood amongst the china plates and the cuddly toys.

"Wow!" whispered Nathan, diving into the shop.

A bell jangled above his head, and a voice from the back room called, "Won't be a moment. I'm just making a cup of tea."

Nathan turned towards the cupboard. If only he could sneak a closer look. If only he could count the dragon's legs. He stuffed the cough sweets into his pocket, glanced over his shoulder and climbed into the window display. Then, very gently, he touched the scaly tail.

There came a soft sound like a wind-chime on a summer day, and almost at once the cupboard doors swung open. Nathan peered inside and gasped.

Someone was smiling at him. Someone whose clothes looked like silky red pyjamas, and whose hair was the colour of midnight.

"Welcome to the Dragon Doorway, Nathan," said a girl's voice. "I am Ling, the Great Magician's daughter. I've been waiting for you." And with that, she pulled him inside the cupboard.

"Wait!" yelped Nathan. "You can't— I can't—"

But the door had already slammed behind him, and darkness swirled down like smoke. A second later lights flashed around his head, and the whole world began to spin.

"Help!" he wailed. "This is worse than the Ride of Fear at the fair." The floor swooped horribly, tilted, settled itself and became suddenly still.

Ling threw open the door, and a stream of daylight stung Nathan's eyes. "Where are we?" he groaned.

"The right place," answered Ling. "At the right time. January has become February. Happy New Year, Nathan!"

"How can you have New Year in February?" grumbled Nathan, who still felt rather wobbly.

Ling giggled and dragged him outside. "In my country, the old year only ends when the new moon arrives," she said.

They were standing in the middle of a market, but it was nothing like the one at home. Crowds of people stretched in all directions.

The air buzzed with excitement and the stalls seemed to be hung with rainbows. There were kites and banners, lanterns and fans, paper flowers and shimmering robes. Huge masks grinned like friendly monsters, and people carried tiny trees shaped like lollipops.

"Kumquat trees," said Ling with a smile. "Orange fruits are lucky here, especially if you eat an even number."

"Help yourself," said Nathan, holding out the bag of kumquats. "But is it safe to leave the Dragon Doorway here?"

"Of course." Ling closed the door firmly
and ran her fingers down the dragon's tail. "It
belongs to the Great Magician." Then she took
two kumquats and hurried away.

Nathan scurried after her. He wished he knew
where she was going. He wished he knew where
he was.

Ling's flame-coloured jacket flickered ahead of
Nathan like a firefly, and he hardly had time to
look around. Yet he noticed the clatter of metal
pans and the tangy smells of sizzling food.
"Sweet and spicy," he murmured to himself.
"A bit like the Chinese take-away at home, but
a hundred times nicer..."

27

Oh! That was it! He was in China!

"Stop!" cried Ling, as Nathan crashed into her. "What do you hear now?"

At first, there was just a jumble of noise. Far-away laughter, a baby crying, the trill of a bird. Then he caught a faint pattering that sounded like the dance of tiny skeletons.

Ling twisted him round, and Nathan saw four men seated at a table. They were playing a game with small, white tiles that looked like dominoes. And they were concentrating so hard that Nathan could feel his own skin tingle.

"*Mah Jong*," whispered Ling, dragging him away. "The name means 'Sparrow', and fortunes can be won and lost by the end of a game."

"I see," said Nathan, as the click of the little white tiles grew fainter. "So I've found the 'Land of the Twittering Sparrows.'"

"You have," agreed Ling. "And now it's time to find my father."

Ling led Nathan up a narrow stairway and into
a high room with gleaming windows. Everything
was incredibly neat and clean. Nathan
remembered the muddle in his own house –
Little Maggie's toys all over the floor, a basket of
washing in the kitchen, the tattered remains of
the Christmas decorations still waiting to be
put away.

"Wow!" he said. "Does it always look this tidy?"

"My grandmother has been very busy," smiled Ling. "It's Chinese New Year, so our home must be spotless for the Kitchen God. All the bad spirits are swept outside with the dust and the cobwebs, and we guard the front door with fire-crackers."

Nathan looked back and saw strings of red tubes dangling by the doorway.

"They're only pretend," giggled Ling. "But the bad spirits don't know that, and they're really afraid of loud bangs."

"Afraid of me, too!" boomed a fierce voice.

Nathan spun round to see a tall figure with a long, narrow beard looming over him. The man wore rich robes, beautifully embroidered with exotic animals. It was the Great Magician!

Nathan didn't know what to say, so he bowed very low and held his breath.

"Welcome, my child," cried a softer voice, "You must be hungry after your long voyage."

32

And into the room bustled an old lady
carrying a dish of small brown cakes. The steam
tickled Nathan's nose and his mouth started to
water.

"Try them," said Ling. "Grandmother's
sticky rice-cakes will bring you happiness in
the New Year."

"They're delicious," mumbled Nathan with
his mouth full. He sipped dark tea from a bowl.

"And you're a brilliant cook," he told Ling's
grandmother. "Is everything lucky in your
house today?"

"Indeed," boomed the Great Magician. "The freshly painted door. Ling's new clothes. And—" Sparks shot from his fingertips and he produced a thin, red packet out of the air.

"The fiery colour is for joy. And the heavy coin inside the envelope is for wealth. Keep it safe."

"I promise," said Nathan, holding the gift tightly. But before he could thank everyone, Ling tugged him out of the door and down the stairs.

The Dancing Lion

It was growing dark outside.

"Hurry," cried Ling, "The best is yet to come."

The new moon hid behind a cloak of shadows as the two children joined an excited swarm of people in the market-place. Ling peered impatiently down the road. "The New Year procession will soon be here," she said, "I can't wait!"

Nathan put the red envelope in his pocket and offered Ling some more kumquats. "Why are your father's clothes covered with animals?" he asked.

Ling licked the kumquat juice from her lips. "In China," she explained, "each year is ruled by one of The Twelve Animals." She closed her eyes and recited their names like a spell, "Rat, Ox, Tiger... Rabbit, Dragon, Snake... Horse, Ram, Monkey... Rooster, Dog and Pig. And they're all wonderful, in their own way."

Nathan whistled. "Wow! What a list! But why are they so important?"

"Because they rule us, too. My father was born in the Year of the Dragon. That's why he's so marvellous. And I'm a Monkey," said Ling with a grin. "Which means that I'm clever and full of fun."

"I hope I'm a Tiger," growled Nathan, but Ling shook her head.

"You're a Horse," she said firmly. "And that means you're about to be very lucky indeed. Look out – here they are!"

And there they were.

Drums thundered, cymbals crashed, acrobats soared like birds – and a dragon appeared. An enormous, silky dragon with scores of scampering legs. It rippled past Nathan, rolling its eyes and blowing smoke from its mouth. "The men inside it practise all year," shouted Ling. "It's supposed to frighten the demons away, and it's much trickier than it looks."

"And there's my dancing lion," yelled Nathan.

"It's big and bouncy like a pantomime cow. No wonder it brings good fortune."

So now there was only one piece of the puzzle to solve. *The Name of the Future.*

A great cheer rose from the crowd, and Nathan found himself gazing at the most marvellous creature of all. A beautiful horse with a golden mane and a swishing, scarlet tail.

The final answer!

"This is *my year!*" cried Nathan joyfully. "The Year of the Horse!"

The Journey Home

Fireworks burst across the sky like autumn flowers, the parade ended, and people called to each other, "*Kung Hei Fat Choy!*" – Hope you grow rich!

Everyone was smiling, and Nathan felt sorry to leave. But he knew it was time to return to the Dragon Doorway.

When they reached the cupboard, Nathan watched Ling stroke the golden scales once more, and then he stepped into the darkness.

"Goodbye!" he called. "*Kung Hei Fat Choy!*
And thank you!"

"*Kung Hei Fat Choy,*" cried Ling, as the door
closed and the market-place spun away.

When the floor settled, Nathan thought he
could still see his friend grinning at him, but the
pale face was his own reflection in a dusty
mirror. He pushed the door and found himself
tumbling out of an ordinary, battered old
wardrobe in the charity shop's window display.

"Good grief!" squawked the woman at the counter, spilling her tea. "Where did you spring from?"

"Sorry," said Nathan, handing her the last two kumquats. "Try these. They're lucky, you know." And he raced away before she could catch her breath.

The Year of the Horse

Once or twice, Nathan wondered if he had fallen asleep in the charity shop and dreamed it all. But when he opened the Great Magician's envelope and dropped the strange, bronze coin in his palm, he knew this was going to be his lucky year.

So when Nathan won a family ticket for the February Mystery Tour, he wasn't really surprised. He wasn't even surprised when Quester's Quality Coach Company took them to a part of London called Chinatown.

Everything looked familiar. Excited crowds lined the streets for the New Year procession.

The new moon hid behind a cloak of shadows as children danced about in their best red clothes. There were paper dragons for sale, and the flash of fire-crackers in the air. Shop fronts were hung with golden lanterns, and people nibbled bags of kumquats.

A kindly stallholder handed Little Maggie a sticky rice-cake, and Nathan suddenly realized that his whole family was smiling. "Happy New Year!" he cried. "Here they are!"

And there they were.

Drums and cymbals. Animals and acrobats. Rippling dragons and dancing lions.

"This is the life," said Dad. "Hey, I think my foot feels better."

"This is fun," said Mum. "I think our luck has changed at last."

"Horsie! Horsie!" laughed Little Maggie, clapping her hands with delight.

A beautiful horse, its coat as glossy as sugar, its mane and tail threaded with bright ribbons, pranced by like a ballet dancer.

And now Nathan *was* surprised.

Waving at him from the horse's high saddle was a girl with hair the colour of midnight. "*Kung Hei Fat Choy*, Nathan!" she called.

"Happy New Year, Ling!" yelled Nathan. But the girl and the horse had already vanished into the crowd. Like a dream. Like magic. Like the old year. After all, she was the Great Magician's daughter.

Glossary

Fire-crackers Bright red fireworks that burst with a bang. Fake fire-crackers are hung around doorways, to frighten away bad spirits.

Kitchen God He is the god of the home, and he likes everything to be neat and clean, especially the oven. Just before the new moon, he visits Heaven to report on his family. At New Year, his family welcomes him home again.

Kumquat A small orange fruit with an edible skin. In China, they are believed to be lucky.

Kung Hei Fat Choy This means, "May you grow rich!" In China, this is the traditional New Year's greeting.

Mah Jong This is a Chinese game played with rectangular tiles, like dominoes. The name means "Sparrow", and the rules are a bit like "Happy Families". *Mah Jong* is still a popular gambling game.

Red clothes Red is the colour of happiness in China. People like to wear this colour to greet the New Year.

Sticky rice-cake This is a special type of food, cooked at New Year, and called *nin go*.

The Twelve Animals The Chinese horoscope has a twelve-year cycle, and each year is ruled by one animal. The animals also rule the people who are born in their special year.